SCIENCE TALES

BIOME BATTLES Book 3

War Over the Wetlands

by Bob Temple   illustrated by Savannah Horrocks

PICTURE WINDOW BOOKS
Minneapolis, Minnesota

Editor: Jill Kalz
Designers: Nathan Gassman and Hilary Wacholz
Page Production: Michelle Biedscheid
Associate Managing Editor: Christianne Jones
The illustrations in this book were created
with watercolor and ink.

Picture Window Books
5115 Excelsior Boulevard
Suite 232
Minneapolis, MN 55416
877-845-8392
www.picturewindowbooks.com

Library of Congress Cataloging-in-Publication Data
Temple, Bob.
War over the wetlands / by Bob Temple ;
illustrated by Savannah Horrocks.
p. cm. — (Read-it! chapter books: Biome Battles ; 3)
ISBN 978-1-4048-3649-5 (library binding)
[1. Wetlands—Fiction. 2. Prophecies—Fiction.
3. Adventure and adventurers—Fiction. 4. Youths'
art.] I. Horrocks, Savannah, 1985- ill. II. Title.
PZ7.T243War 2008
[Fic]—dc22   2007033079

Table of Contents

War Over the Wetlands

A curious boy who many Imps believe is one of the two humans mentioned in the Imp Prophecy

Ari

Ari's best friend and co-adventurer who many Imps believe is the other human from the Imp Prophecy

Kendra

Troll King

Leader of the Trolls, a group of large, mean, smelly creatures who seek to rule the world by destroying the biomes and turning Earth into a wasteland

Tundra

Rain Forest

Desert

4

MAP and CHARACTER KEY

Trace — Son of King Crag, the Imp King, and Ari and Kendra's guide through the world's biomes

King Crag — Leader of the Imps, a group of small, gentle creatures who protect all of Earth's biomes from harm

Prairie

Wetlands

Ocean

IMP VILLAGE

Midnight Surprise

A cool gust of wind woke Ari from a deep sleep. He was tired from a long summer day of playing baseball with friends. He rolled over onto his stomach and leaned up on his elbows. He peered out the window above his headboard.

6

It was a clear night. The moon was bright and low in the sky.

Ari reached up to close the window, hoping to shut out the wind. SMACK! His hand banged into the glass. The window was already closed. So where had the wind come from?

Most boys would probably have decided it was a dream and gone back to sleep. However, Ari's amazing experiences told him it was something else.

Many strange things had happened in Ari's bedroom since he had heard the noises in his closet—a knock, a click, a whistle. A knock, a click, a whistle. At first, Ari thought he was imagining things. His friend Kendra thought he was crazy. But one day Ari finally met the small, shadowy creature who was making the noises.

The creature's name was Trace.

After that, Ari went from worrying about the cause of the strange happenings in his bedroom to hoping they would return. So, when a gust of wind woke him in the middle of the night, Ari's first thought was that Trace, his Imp friend, was returning.

If Trace were back, it was because the Imps needed help. Ari's mind flashed to the battles he had helped fight against the evil Trolls. He thought of the importance of winning those battles, too. Earth's future was at stake.

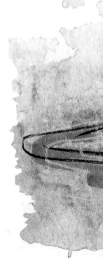

The Trolls lived underground. Unable to survive in sunlight, clean air, and water, they sought to destroy the planet's biomes— to make Earth a wasteland. They could then rise to the surface and

8

take control of Earth.

Ari scooted to the edge of the bed. He was ready to find some answers, even if it took all night.

As he jumped to his feet, Ari heard a sound that gave him his first clue: SPLASH!

Getting Kendra

Water! Ari's bedroom floor was covered with it. The water was about an inch deep. And it was cold.

10

Right away, Ari knew the water was another signal from the Imps. It had to be. After all, Ari's bedroom was on the second floor. Only a horrible flood could reach that high, and Ari knew that wasn't the case.

Ari had to get Kendra. All of his adventures with the Imps had included Kendra. The Imps believed that Ari and Kendra were the two humans from the Imp Prophecy. The prophecy said that two young humans would come to help the Imps in their battle to save Earth. Together, they would overcome the Trolls once and for all.

Getting Kendra to come over in the middle of the night wasn't going to be easy. But Ari knew this couldn't wait until morning. Soon Trace would appear, and Ari needed to have Kendra by his side.

Ari quickly changed clothes. He moved toward his bedroom door and opened it.

The door swept through the water, sending little ripples toward the far wall. Ari stepped out into the hallway on his toes. The hallway was dry.

Ari walked as quickly and softly as he could across the wood floor. He tried to stay away from the boards that creaked. He didn't want to wake his mom.

He tiptoed down the stairs and slipped outside. Then he leapt off the front porch and ran for Kendra's house a block away.

Running through the moonlight, Ari was

there in a flash. He rushed around to the back of the house and looked up at Kendra's bedroom window. It was closed.

Ari gathered up a few sticks and pebbles and tossed them toward the window. Each one bounced off the glass.

A few seconds later, Ari saw a rustling behind the window.

Kendra slid the window open and poked her head out. "Ari! What are you doing?" she asked. "Are you crazy? It's the middle of the night. I'm trying to sleep!"

Ari waved for her to come down. "Come on!" he whispered. "I think we've got work to do!"

A Wet World

Kendra's face lit up. She shut the window and disappeared into her room. A moment later, she ran out the back door.

15

"OK, what's going on?" she asked.

"Trace must be coming for us," Ari said. "My bedroom floor is soaked. You have to see it."

The kids hurried back to Ari's house. Wild thoughts ran through their heads as they tried to figure out what this adventure might bring. One thing was certain—it had something to do with water.

Ari led the way inside and up the stairs. When he and Kendra reached the top, they peered down the hallway toward Ari's bedroom door.

Whoosh! There he was! The shadowy creature whizzed through Ari's bedroom door, out of sight. Ari turned to Kendra. They both smiled. They knew who that was—Trace.

The two kids crept down the hallway. Ari paused in front of his door and caught

his breath. Kendra reached over and put her hand on his shoulder.

"Ready?" she asked nervously.

"Yeah," Ari said. "Let's go."

Ari turned the doorknob and slowly pushed open the door. Just as had happened in their other adventures, Ari's room was no longer there.

Instead, lying before them was a dark, watery land: a wetland.

CHAPTER 3

Ari and Kendra didn't wait. They knew just what to do. Without a word, they stepped through the doorway and sank deep into the murky swamp. When Ari closed the door behind them, his bedroom and his house disappeared.

Once again, Ari and Kendra were in a new biome. A new adventure was about to begin.

4

A Worried Friend

Ari and Kendra struggled to walk through the swamp. Their feet sank deep into the thick mud.

All around them, flying insects whirred,

buzzed, and hummed. Frogs croaked. Crickets chirped. Once in a while, the water rippled, bubbled, or splashed. The kids wondered what creatures were swimming around them.

More importantly, they wondered when they were going to see their friend Trace. He was the one who had led them to this new place. They hoped he would soon come to greet them.

"Maybe we should just find a dry spot and wait for Trace," Ari said.

"No way," Kendra said. "I'm not standing still. It's the middle of the night, Ari. You know who comes out in the middle of the night, right?"

"Trolls," they said together.

"OK, let's keep moving," Ari said. "Who knows? Maybe we'll find the Imp village before Trace finds us."

The words were barely out of his mouth when a small, dark figure flashed by Ari's side. Just as quickly, it was gone. A moment later, another flash was followed by a splash directly in front of them.

It was Trace.

He looked just like always: a small, boyish creature with long, dark hair, pointed ears, and bright eyes that twinkled.

The Imp smiled as he reached for Kendra's hand.

"Where are we?" Kendra asked.

Trace shook his head, and the kids nodded. They quickly remembered a truth about Imps—they can speak only inside the Imp village.

Trace led Ari and Kendra through the murky swamp to the wall of the village. Once there, Trace took both of their hands and walked directly toward the stones. At the moment when Ari and Kendra felt sure they would smack into the wall, they walked through it.

Inside the Imp village, trees and giant flowers swayed in the breeze. A thin, sparkling waterfall poured straight from the clouds into the village center. Tiny Imps scurried and flew around on their nighttime chores. A few of them sang. It felt safe and warm, like home.

Looking down the hill, Ari spotted the home of King Crag, Trace's father. He wondered how the king would greet them this time. The king didn't believe in the Imp Prophecy. He didn't want Ari and Kendra's help. Ari never felt very comfortable around him.

The rest of the Imps, however, welcomed Ari and Kendra each time they came. Sometimes, they even whistled and cheered.

Trace let go of the kids' hands and turned to face them. Since they were now inside the walls, he could speak.

"My father ... he does not know you are here," Trace said. "The Trolls ... they are here in the wetland. We do not know what they are planning to do, but we know it will be bad."

"What's happening?" Kendra asked. "How can we help?"

Trace looked over his shoulder and grew more nervous with every word. "Yesterday," he said, "I saw them."

"Trolls?" Ari asked.

"No, it is worse," Trace said, trembling. "Much worse."

"What could possibly be worse than Trolls?" Kendra asked.

"Trogs," Trace said.

Trogs

Ari and Kendra weren't sure what to say. They had never heard of a Trog. Trace stared up at them as if they should know.

Finally, Ari spoke. "Trogs?" he said. "What's a Trog?"

"They are hideous," Trace said. "Part Troll, part frog. They are as big as a Troll—and just as smelly, too. But they can leap like frogs and snatch up things with their sticky tongues."

"And are they … evil?" Kendra asked.

"No, not usually," Trace said. "But they can be, especially if evil beings gain control of them."

"And you believe that the Trolls have taken control of the Trogs," Ari said.

Trace nodded.

"How do you know this?" Ari asked.

"I heard the Troll king talking to them just last night," Trace said. "He was training them for an attack. He wants the Trogs to attack during the day, so the Trolls can come out at night to finish the job."

"Attack?" Kendra said. "Attack who?"

"Attack us!" Trace said. "The Trogs can leap our village walls. They will gobble us up and—"

Trace stopped short. He couldn't bring himself to say it.

"Then there will be no one to stop the Trolls from destroying the wetland," Ari said, finishing Trace's thoughts. "Once they've

done that, there will be nothing to stop them from controlling the entire planet."

Ari, Kendra, and Trace stood silently for a moment. They could feel the danger growing. Dawn broke over the walls of the Imp village. With the first peek of sunlight came the first of dozens and dozens of hideous creatures.

The Trogs were attacking!

The first Trog leapt into the village with ease. Its huge, bulging eyes darted from side to side. It was as big as a Troll, with long arms that dragged on the ground like a Troll's. But its back legs were all frog. It leapt easily and forcefully.

In an instant, the Trog snapped up an Imp with its tongue and bounded back over the village wall.

Imps scattered as more Trogs cleared the walls. Some Imps tried to fly away. But the sticky tongues of the Trogs quickly snapped them up, too.

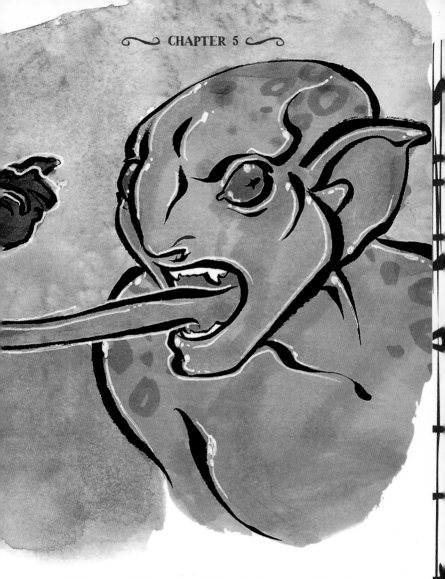

Ari headed for the king's house. He knew the Trogs would want to capture King Crag.

Kendra and Trace quickly found a hiding place in some bushes near the village wall.

There, they watched as hundreds of Trogs snatched up Imp after Imp.

Ari neared the king's house and reached for the door. But suddenly, a giant Trog's tongue wrapped around his waist and lifted him off the ground. The creature rolled its eyes from side to side and then leapt over the village wall.

Kendra struggled not to yell after her friend. It was important that she stay quiet. She and Trace were now Ari's only hope.

Trace grabbed Kendra's hand and pulled her through the wall. The two of them ran after the Trog as it bounced away through the wetland with Ari.

Sunken Hero

Ari struggled in the Trog's sticky grip. Finally, he got one leg free and kicked the creature in the eye. The Trog let go, and Ari fell toward the wetland.

There was nothing Ari could do but hope for a soft landing.

SPLASH!

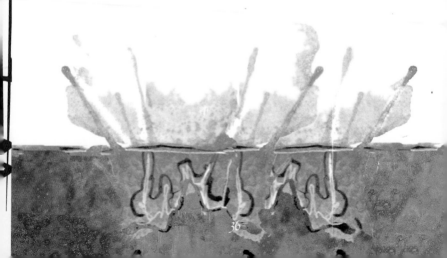

Kendra gasped as Ari hit the water. She started to run toward him, but Trace grabbed her arm and pulled her back behind a tree. Kendra knew that Trace was just trying to protect her. If she went after Ari, she too would be gobbled up. But it was difficult to stand there and do nothing.

Kendra and Trace watched for signs of life in the water, but there were none—no splashing, no movement at all. Ari was underwater. Gone.

*

The hard landing had stunned Ari, and he sank to the bottom of the wetland. When he had gathered his senses, he saw the giant webbed feet of a Trog hopping in and out of the water. Ari knew the Trog was looking for him, so he tried to stay down.

I have to hold my breath as long as I can, he thought.

The Trog bounced around a few more times, then bounced away for good. Ari relaxed, knowing he had fooled the Trog into thinking he was dead.

Ari started to put together a plan. Should he head back to the Imp village to try to battle the Trogs that were still there? Or should he follow the Trogs that had already left to see where they were taking the Imps? Where could he do the most good?

Suddenly, Ari realized something shocking: He wasn't holding his breath anymore! He sat motionless for a moment, unsure of what was going on. In the quiet of the underwater world, Ari noticed his chest moving up and down. He was breathing below the surface of the water. He was breathing ... underwater!

Ari couldn't believe it. He started to swim around the wetland. He swam along the water's surface. He glided in between pond lilies and clumps of cattails. He swam close to the muddy bottom, where turtles fed on snails and insects, and he swam everywhere in between.

With his eyes open, Ari could see clearly in the murky water. He never struggled to breathe.

As he swam among the fish, happily practicing his new skill, he seemed to forget about the trouble on the land around him. Before he could get too relaxed, however, he ran into an unwelcome surprise.

There, staring straight at him, was a Trog.

7

Fighting Back

Kendra began to cry. It was not like her to show emotion like that, but she was certain her friend was dead.

What would she do without Ari? How would the Imp Prophecy ever be fulfilled, now that he was gone?

Trace wasted little time. He grabbed Kendra's hand and pulled her back into the village. Once inside, the pair sprinted to a

nearby cave. They dived through the narrow opening, dodging the Trogs' tongues. There they found a welcome surprise.

"Father!" Trace yelled.

It was King Crag. He, too, had found safety in the cave.

"My son," the king said, "the Trogs have turned against us. I am afraid they will destroy us all!"

"I know," Trace said. "But I have a plan." Then Trace turned to Kendra and asked, "Did you see what Ari did when he fought the Trog? He kicked its eye, Kendra. The Trogs' greatest weakness is their eyes. We must attack their giant eyes!"

Kendra quickly grabbed some rocks and moved toward the entrance. A sticky tongue flashed in at her. As it pulled back, she chased it. When she caught her first glimpse of the Trog's eyes, she hit one with a rock.

The Trog let out a horrible groan. It tumbled backward, reaching for its eye. Then it stumbled and headed for the village wall, clearing it in a single leap. Kendra heard the Trog croak in pain all of the way.

45

Trace and the king followed Kendra's lead. Other Imps, seeing Kendra's example, began throwing whatever they could find. Slowly but steadily, Kendra and the Imps regained control. The Trogs bounded out of the village, heading for safety.

*

Ari saw the splashes of dozens of Trogs in the water around him. Still, his gaze never left the Trog that was staring at him. This Trog seemed smaller—perhaps younger—than the ones who had attacked the Imp village. Still, its large, bulging eyes made it look scary.

"You're not a Trog," the creature said suddenly. "What's your name?" The voice was high and soft. It made Ari think the Trog was a young girl.

"Ari," he said. "And no, I'm not a Trog. I'm a human."

"No, you're not," she said, darting around him. "Humans can't swim like you can. They can't breathe underwater, either. What kind of creature *are* you?"

Ari didn't know what to say. She was right. Humans can't do what he was doing. Yet he knew he was, in fact, human. Or was he?

"You're right," Ari said. "Humans can't do this."

"Well, I don't know what you are," she said. "I don't really care, as long as you're not an Imp. My mother says we Trogs hate the Imps."

Ari and the young Trog talked underwater for a long time. Ari tried to find out why the Trogs wanted to help the Trolls. The young Trog didn't seem to know. Ari hoped to learn more about the Trogs, find out where they had taken the captured Imps, and figure out a way to help the Imps in the process.

As the day wound down, Ari worried about Kendra and the Imps. He hadn't seen any of them in hours.

49

Night was coming, and that meant one thing: The Trolls would be free to roam the surface of the wetland biome.

Suddenly, two huge Trog feet landed in the water very near to Ari. In an instant, Ari and the young Trog were snatched up out of the water by two giant Trog hands.

Trogs Unite

The creature that now held Ari easily in one hand was the biggest Trog of them all.

"Phibi!" he shouted. "What are you doing, talking to this ... this thing?"

Before the young Trog could answer, the giant Trog dropped her and pulled Ari closer to his face. His huge eyes stared at Ari. Ari was afraid he was about to become a meal.

"Who are you?" the giant Trog asked. "How did you come to this place? Why do you help the Imps?"

Ari struggled for the words. There wasn't a simple answer for all of these questions. "They ... they chose me," Ari said, "to help them save the world."

The giant Trog let out a laugh. "The Imps? Save the world?" he said. "Ha! Only the Trolls can save the world. When the Trolls are in power, the world will be safe."

Even though he was dangling high in the air, Ari still found the courage to yell. "No!" he said. "That's not true! The Trolls are lying to you! I've seen what they're doing. The Trolls want to rule the world by destroying it first. When the Imps are gone, the Trolls will destroy your wetland. Then where will you live?"

The giant Trog gave Ari a puzzled look.

Behind him, the sun was setting.

Trolls began to rise to the surface. With no Imps to protect the land, they started to destroy the biome.

"Bring out the pumps!" the Troll king yelled in the distance. "Remove this water! When the land is dry, burn the reeds!"

The giant Trog dropped quickly underwater. He continued to hold Ari, but the look on his face changed. He peeked above the waterline and saw a group of Trolls setting up pumps. He saw another group carrying tree saws and shovels.

"Gather up the other Trogs," Ari suggested. "Tell them the truth. You have to stop the Trolls before it's too late!"

The giant Trog paused. Then, he stood up straight, tightened his grip on Ari, and bounced away. The Trolls ignored him. They believed he was on their side.

The giant Trog brought Ari to an island in the middle of the swamp. He explained the situation to a group of Trog guards there. They nodded and bounded off.

"The Imp prisoners are locked in a hollow bald cypress at the end of this path," the giant Trog said to Ari. "Here's the key. Now, go!"

Ari ran down the path as the giant Trog headed off to battle the Trolls. Ari could see the tree just off in the distance. The closer he got, the more he smiled. There, already setting the Imps free, were Kendra, Trace, and King Crag.

"Ari!" Kendra yelled. "You're alive!"

"Kendra, I have so much to tell you," Ari said. "You won't believe what I can do!"

Off in the distance, the booming sounds of battle began. Trolls roared and snarled. The ground shook. The water around the island sloshed and gurgled. With a nod to their king, the newly freed Imps flew off to join in the battle.

CHAPTER 8

57

But the battle didn't last long. The Trolls were no match for the nimble Trogs. They quickly scattered. Dozens of Trolls soon arrived at the prison tree. They were carried on the tongues and in the hands of the

Trogs. Trace and his father happily opened the door to let the captured Trolls inside.

Trace then took the hands of his human friends and smiled. Ari and Kendra knew it was time for them to return home.

The three of them walked away without saying a word. The only sounds were the sloshing of their feet through the wet, muddy swamp.

Soon they saw Ari's bedroom door. Trace easily walked Ari and Kendra through it, into the hallway.

There was a twinkle in Trace's eyes as he nodded his thanks to his human friends. He held Ari's hand tightly, forcing a crumpled piece of paper into his palm. Just as he had done before, he winked and disappeared through Ari's door.

Ari opened the piece of paper. He held it close to his eyes. In the dim hallway, he read the backward words aloud:

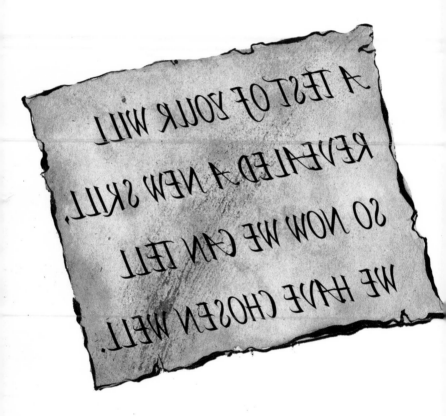

AFTERWORD

What Is a Wetland?
Wetlands are regions of land that are covered with water at least part of the year. They have very wet soil and are home to many water-loving plants. Wetlands can be found all over the world. Marshes, swamps, and bogs are three types of wetlands. Wetland water can be fresh, salty, or mixed.

Wetland Plants and Animals
Because wetlands have areas of standing water and very wet soil, water plants grow well there. Examples include pond lilies, cattails, mosses, and duckweed. Some wetlands also include bald cypress trees, gum trees, and green ash trees.

Wetlands are home to a large number of animal species. Frogs, toads, and other amphibians live there. So do reptiles such as turtles, snakes, and alligators, and mammals such as otters, beavers, and deer. Wetlands are also home to geese, ducks, flamingos, and many other birds. There are also many insects, such as flies and mosquitoes.

Why Are Wetlands Important?
Wetlands near the seashore protect the areas around them from storms. They absorb the force of strong winds and waves. Wetlands also help to take out, or filter, pollutants that can get into the water. Wetlands act like sponges, controlling water levels during times of flooding.

Wetlands also provide protected areas for fish and shellfish to lay eggs. They provide people with the chance to hunt, fish, bird watch, and photograph wildlife.

GLOSSARY
bald cypress—a large wetland tree with flat, needlelike
leaves and a broad-based trunk
biome—a large geographical area with its own distinct
animals, plants, climate, and geography; there are six
biomes on Earth: desert, grassland (including savannas
and prairies), ocean, rain forest, tundra, and wetlands
reeds—tall grasses that grow especially well in wet areas
species—a group of animals or plants that has many
things in common
swamp—a type of wetland with many trees and shrubs
wetland—an area that has very wet soil and is covered with
water at least part of the year

ON THE WEB
FactHound offers a safe, fun way to find Web sites related
to topics in this book. All of the sites on FactHound have
been researched by our staff.

1. Visit *www.facthound.com*
2. Type in this special code: 1404836497
3. Click on the FETCH IT button.

Your trusty FactHound will fetch the best sites for you!

LOOK FOR ALL OF THE BOOKS
IN THE SCIENCE TALES SERIES:
Rescuing the Rain Forest (Book 1)
Taking Back the Tundra (Book 2)
War Over the Wetlands (Book 3)
Danger in the Desert (Book 4)
Protecting the Prairie (Book 5)
Operation Ocean (Book 6)